THE MARQUISE OF O–

HEINRICH VON KLEIST

THE MARQUISE OF O—

TRANSLATED BY
DAVID LUKE AND NIGEL REEVES

PENGUIN BOOKS

PENGUIN BOOKS

Published by the Penguin Group

Penguin Books USA Inc., 375 Hudson Street,
New York, New York 10014, U.S.A.
Penguin Books Ltd, 27 Wrights Lane,
London W8 5TZ, England
Penguin Books Australia Ltd, Ringwood,
Victoria, Australia
Penguin Books Canada Ltd, 10 Alcorn Avenue,
Toronto, Ontario, Canada M4V 3B2
Penguin Books (N.Z.) Ltd, 182–190 Wairau Road,
Auckland 10, New Zealand

Penguin Books Ltd, Registered Offices:
Harmondsworth, Middlesex, England

Published in Penguin Books 1995

This translation of "The Marquise of O" appears in *The Marquise of O and Other Stories* by Heinrich von Kleist, translated and introduced by David Luke and Nigel Reeves, published by Penguin Books.

ISBN 0 14 60.0187 7

Printed in the United States of America

In M—, an important town in northern Italy, the widowed
Marquise of O—, a lady of unblemished reputation and the
mother of several well-brought-up children, inserted the following announcement in the newspapers: that she had, without knowledge of the cause, come to find herself in a certain
situation; that she would like the father of the child she was
expecting to disclose his identity to her; and that she was resolved, out of consideration for her family, to marry him.
The lady who, under the constraint of unalterable circumstances, had with such boldness taken so strange a step and
thus exposed herself to the derision of society, was the
daughter of Colonel G—, the Commandant of the citadel at
M—. About three years earlier her husband, the Marquis of
O—, to whom she was most deeply and tenderly attached,
had lost his life in the course of a journey to Paris on family
business. At the request of her excellent mother she had, after
his death, left the country estate at V— where she had lived
hitherto, and had returned with her two children to the
house of her father the Commandant. Here she had for the
next few years lived a very secluded life, devoted to art and
reading, the education of her children and the care of her
parents, until the — War suddenly filled the neighbourhood

with the armed forces of almost all the powerful European states, including those of Russia. Colonel G——, who had orders to defend the citadel, told his wife and daughter to withdraw either to the latter's country estate or to that of his son, which was near V——. But before the ladies had even concluded their deliberations, weighing up the hardships to which they would be subject in the fortress against the horrors to which they would be exposed in the open country, the Russian troops were already besieging the citadel and calling upon it to surrender. The Colonel announced to his family that he would now simply act as if they were not present, and answered the Russians with bullets and grenades. The enemy replied by shelling the citadel. They set fire to the magazine, occupied an outwork, and when after a further call to surrender the Commandant still hesitated to do so, an attack was mounted during the night and the fortress taken by storm.

Just as the Russian troops, covered by heavy artillery fire, were forcing their way into the castle, the left wing of the Commandant's residence was set ablaze and the women were forced to leave. The Colonel's wife, hurrying after her daughter who was fleeing downstairs with her children, called out to her that they should all stay together and take refuge in the cellars below; but at that very moment a grenade exploding inside the house threw everything into complete confusion. The Marquise found herself, with her two children, in the outer precincts of the castle where fierce fighting was already in progress and shots flashed through the darkness, driving her back again into the burning building, panic-stricken and with no idea where to turn. Here, just as she was trying to escape through the back door, she had the misfortune to encounter a troop of enemy riflemen, who as soon as they saw her suddenly fell silent, slung their guns over their shoulders and, with obscene gestures, seized her and carried her off. In vain she screamed for help to her terrified women, who went fleeing back through the gate, as the dreadful rabble tugged her hither and thither, fighting among themselves. Dragging her into the innermost courtyard they began to assault her in the most shameful way, and she was just about to sink to the ground when a Russian officer, hearing her piercing screams, appeared on the scene and with furious blows of his sword drove the dogs back from the prey for which they lusted. To the Marquise he seemed an angel sent from heaven. He smashed the hilt of his sword into the face of one of the murderous brutes, who still had his arms round her slender waist, and the man reeled back with blood pouring from his mouth; he then addressed the lady politely in French, offered her his arm and led her into the other wing of the palace which the flames had not yet reached and where, having already been stricken speechless by her ordeal, she now collapsed in a dead faint. Then—the officer instructed the Marquise's frightened servants, who presently arrived, to send for a doctor; he assured them that she would soon recover, replaced his hat and returned to the fighting.

In a short time the fortress had been completely taken by the enemy; the Commandant, who had only continued to defend it because he had not been offered amnesty, was withdrawing to the main gate with dwindling strength when the Russian officer, his face very flushed, came out through it and called on him to surrender. The Commandant replied that this demand was all that he had been waiting for, handed over his sword, and asked permission to go into the castle and look for his family. The Russian officer, who to judge by the part he was playing seemed to be one of the leaders of the attack, gave him leave to do so, accompanied by a guard; he then rather hastily took command of a detachment, put an end to the fighting at all points where the issue still seemed to be in doubt, and rapidly garrisoned all the strong points of the citadel. Shortly after this he returned to the scene of action, gave orders for the extinction of the fire which was beginning to spread furiously, and joined in this work himself with heroic exertion when his orders were not carried out with sufficient zeal. At one moment he was climbing about among burning gables with a hose in his hand, directing the jet of water at the flame; the next moment, while his Asiatic compatriots stood appalled, he would be right inside the arsenals rolling out powder kegs and live grenades. Meanwhile the Commandant had entered the house and learned with utter consternation of the misadventure which had befallen his daughter. The Marquise, who without medical assistance had already completely recovered from her fainting fit, as the Russian officer had predicted, was so overjoyed to see all her family alive and well that she stayed in bed only in deference to their excessive solicitude, assuring her father that all she wanted was to be allowed to get up and thank her rescuer. She had already been told that he was Count F—, Lieutenant-Colonel of the — Rifle Corps and Knight of an Order of Merit and of various orders. She asked her father to request him most urgently not to leave the citadel without paying them a short call in the residential quarters. The Commandant, approving his daughter's feelings, did indeed return immediately to the fortifications and found the Count hurrying to and fro, busy with a multitude of military tasks; there being no better opportunity to do so, he spoke to him on the ramparts where he was reviewing his injured and disorganized soldiery. Here he conveyed his grateful daughter's message, and Count F— assured him that he was only waiting for a moment's respite from his business to come and pay her his respects. He was in the act of inquiring about the lady's health when several officers came up with reports which snatched him back again into the turmoil of war. At daybreak the general in command of the Russian forces arrived and inspected the citadel. He complimented the Commandant, expressed his regret that the latter's courage had not been better matched by good fortune, and granted him permission, on his word of honour, to go to whatever place he chose. The Commandant thanked him warmly, and declared that the past twenty-four hours had given him much reason to be grateful to the Russians in general and in particular to young Count F—, Lieutenant-Colonel of the — Rifle Corps. The general asked what had happened, and when he was told of the criminal assault on the Commandant's daughter, his indignation knew no bounds. He called Count F— forward by name and, after a brief speech commending him for his gallant behaviour, which caused the Count to blush scarlet, he declared that he would have the perpetrators of this shameful outrage shot for disgracing the name of the Tsar, and ordered the Count to identify them. Count F— replied in some confusion that he was not able to report their names, since the faint glimmer of the lamps in the castle courtyard had made it impossible for him to recognize their faces. The general, who had heard that at the time in question the castle had been on fire, expressed surprise at this, remarking that after all persons known to one could be recognized in the darkness by their voices; the Count could only shrug his shoulders in embarrassment, and the general directed him to investigate the affair with the utmost urgency and rigour. At this moment someone pressed forward through the assembled troops and reported that one of the miscreants wounded by Count F— had collapsed in the corridor, and had been dragged by the Commandant's servants to a cell in which he was still being held prisoner. The general immediately had him brought under guard to his presence, where he was summarily interrogated; the prisoner named his accomplices and the whole rabble, five in number, were then shot. Having dealt with this matter, the general ordered the withdrawal of his troops from the citadel, leaving only a small garrison to occupy it; the officers quickly returned to the various units under their command; amid the confusion of the general dispersal the Count approached the

Commandant and said how very sorry he was that in the circumstances he could do no more than send his respectful compliments to the Marquise; and in less than an hour the whole fortress was again empty of Russian troops.

The family were now considering how they might find a future opportunity of expressing their gratitude to the Count in some way, when they were appalled to learn that on the very day of his departure from the fortress he had lost his life in an encounter with enemy troops. The messenger who brought this news to M— had himself seen him, with a mortal bullet-wound in the chest, being carried to P—, where according to a reliable report he had died just as his bearers were about to set him down. The Commandant, going in person to the post-house to find out further details of what had happened, merely learnt in addition that on the battlefield, at the moment of being hit, he had cried out 'Giulietta! This bullet avenges you!', whereupon his lips had been sealed forever. The Marquise was inconsolable at having missed the opportunity of throwing herself at his feet. She reproached herself bitterly that when he had refused, presumably for reasons of modesty, to come and see her in the castle, she had not gone to him herself; she grieved for the unfortunate lady, bearing the same name as herself, whom he had remembered at the very moment of his death, and made vain efforts to discover her whereabouts in order to tell her of this unhappy and moving event; and several months passed before she herself could forget him.

It was now necessary for the Commandant and his family

to move out of the citadel and let the Russian commander take up residence there. They first considered settling on the Colonel's estate, of which the Marquise was very fond; but since her father did not like living in the country, the family took a house in the town and furnished it suitably as a permanent home. They now reverted entirely to their former way of life. The Marquise resumed the long-interrupted education of her children, taking up where she had left off, and for her leisure hours she again brought out her easel and her books. But whereas she had previously been the very paragon of good health, she now began to be afflicted by repeated indispositions, which would make her unfit for company for weeks at a time. She suffered from nausea, giddiness and fainting fits, and was at a loss to account for her strange condition. One morning, when the family were sitting at tea and her father had left the room for a moment, the Marquise, emerging from a long reverie, said to her mother: 'If any woman were to tell me that she had felt just as I did a moment ago when I picked up this teacup, I should say to myself that she must be with child.' The Commandant's wife said she did not understand, and the Marquise repeated her statement, saying that she had just experienced a sensation exactly similar to those she had had a few years ago when she had been expecting her second daughter. Her mother remarked with a laugh that she would no doubt be giving birth to the god of Fantasy. The Marquise replied in an equally jesting tone that at any rate Morpheus, or one of his attendant dreams, must be the father. But the Colonel returned to the room and the conversation was broken off, and since a few days later the Marquise felt quite herself again, the whole subject was forgotten.

Shortly after this, at a time when the Commandant's son, who was a forestry official, also happened to be at home, a footman entered and to the family's absolute consternation announced Count F—. 'Count F—!' exclaimed the father and his daughter simultaneously; and amazement made them all speechless. The footman assured them that he had seen and heard aright, and that the Count was already standing waiting in the anteroom. The Commandant himself leapt to his feet to open the door to him, and he entered the room, his face a little pale, but looking as beautiful as a young god. When the initial scene of incomprehension and astonishment was over, with the parents objecting that surely he was dead and the Count assuring them that he was alive, he turned to their daughter with a gaze betokening much emotion, and his first words to her were to ask her how she was. The Marquise assured him that she was very well, and only wished to know how he, for his part, had come to life again. The Count, however, would not be diverted, and answered that she could not be telling him the truth: to judge by her complexion, he said, she seemed strangely fatigued, and unless he was very much mistaken she was unwell, and suffering from some indisposition. The Marquise, touched by the sincerity with which he spoke, answered that as a matter of fact this fatigue could, since he insisted, be interpreted as the aftermath of an ailment from which she had suffered a few weeks

9

ago, but that she had no reason to fear that it would be of any consequence. At this he appeared overjoyed, exclaiming: 'Neither have I!'—and then asked her if she would be willing to marry him. The Marquise did not know what to think of this unusual behaviour. Blushing deeply, she looked at her mother, and the latter stared in embarrassment at her son and her husband; meanwhile the Count approached the Marquise and, taking her hand as if to kiss it, asked again whether she had understood his question. The Commandant asked him if he would not be seated, and placed a chair for him, courteously but rather solemnly. The Commandant's wife said: 'Count, we shall certainly go on thinking you are a ghost, until you have explained to us how you rose again from the grave in which you were laid at P—.' The Count, letting go of the young lady's hand, sat down and said that circumstances compelled him to be very brief. He told them that he had been carried to P— mortally wounded in the chest; that there he had despaired of his life for several months; that during this time his every thought had been devoted to the Marquise; that her presence in his mind had caused him an intermingling of delight and pain that was indescribable; that after his recovery he had finally rejoined the army; that he had there been quite unable to set his mind at rest; that he had several times taken up his pen to relieve the agitation of his heart by writing to the Colonel and the Marquise; that he had been suddenly sent to Naples with dispatches; that he did not know whether from there he might not be ordered to go on to Constantinople; that he would

10

perhaps even have to go to St Petersburg; that in the meantime there was a compelling need in his soul, a certain matter which he had to settle if he was to go on living; that as he was passing through M— he had been unable to resist the impulse to take a few steps towards the fulfilment of this purpose; in short, that he deeply desired the happiness of the Marquise's hand in marriage, and that he most respectfully, fervently and urgently begged them to be so kind as to give him their answer on this point. The Commandant, after a long pause, replied that he of course felt greatly honoured by this proposal, if it was meant seriously, as he had no doubt it was. But on the death of her husband, the Marquis of O—, his daughter had resolved not to embark on any second marriage. Since, however, the Count had not long ago put her under so great an obligation, it was not impossible that her decision might thereby be altered in accordance with his wishes; but that for the present he would beg him on her behalf to allow her some little time in which to think the matter over quietly. The Count assured him that these kind words did indeed satisfy all his hopes; that they would in other circumstances even completely content him; that he was very well aware of the great impropriety of finding them insufficient; but that pressing circumstances, which he was not in a position to particularize further, made it extremely desirable that he should have a more definite reply; that the horses that were to take him to Naples were already harnessed to his carriage; and that if there was anything in this house that spoke in his favour—here he glanced at the Marquise—then

11

he would most earnestly implore them not to let him depart without kindly making some declaration to that effect. The Colonel, rather disconcerted by his behaviour, answered that the gratitude the Marquise felt for him certainly justified him in entertaining considerable hopes, but not so great as these; in taking a step on which the happiness of her whole life depended she would not proceed without due circumspection. It was indispensable that his daughter, before committing herself, should have the pleasure of his closer acquaintance. He invited him to return to M— after completing his journey and his business as ordered, and to stay for a time in the family's house as their guest. If his daughter then came to feel that she could hope to find happiness with him—but not until then—he, her father, would be delighted to hear that she had given him a definite answer. The Count, his face reddening, said that during his whole journey here he had predicted to himself that this would be the outcome of his impatient desire; that the distress into which it plunged him was nevertheless extreme; that in view of the unfavourable impression which he knew must be created by the part he was at present being forced to play, closer acquaintance could not fail to be advantageous to him; that he felt he could answer for his reputation, if indeed it was felt necessary to take into account this most dubious of all attributes; that the one ignoble action he had committed in his life was unknown to the world and that he was already taking steps to make amends for it; that, in short, he was a man of honour, and begged them to accept his assurance that this assurance was the truth. The

Commandant, smiling slightly, but without irony, replied that he endorsed all these statements. He had, he said, never yet made the acquaintance of any young man who had in so short a time displayed so many admirable qualities of character. He was almost sure that a short period of further consideration would dispel the indecision that still prevailed; but before the matter had been discussed both with his own son and with the Count's family, he could give no other answer than the one he had already given. To this the Count rejoined that his parents were both dead and he was his own master; his uncle was General K——, whose consent to the marriage he was prepared to guarantee. He added that he possessed a substantial fortune, and was prepared to settle in Italy. The Commandant made him a courteous bow, but repeated that his own wishes were as he had just stated, and requested that this subject should now be dropped until after the Count's journey. The latter, after a short pause in which he showed every sign of a great agitation, remarked, turning to the young lady's mother, that he had done his utmost to avoid being sent on this mission; that he had taken the most decisive possible steps to this end, venturing to approach the Commander-in-Chief as well as his uncle General K——; but that they had thought that this journey would dispel a state of melancholy in which his illness had left him, whereas instead it was now plunging him into utter wretchedness. The family were nonplussed by this statement. The Count, wiping his brow, added that if there were any hope that to do so would bring him nearer to the goal of his wishes, he would try postponing his journey for a day or perhaps even for a little longer. So saying he looked in turn at the Commandant, the Marquise, and her mother. The Commandant cast his eyes down in vexation and did not answer him. His wife said: 'Go, go, my dear Count, make your journey to Naples; on your way back give us for some time the pleasure of your company, and the rest will see to itself.' The Count sat for a moment, seeming to ponder what he should do. Then, rising and setting aside his chair, he said that since the hopes with which he had entered this house had admittedly been over-precipitate and since the family very understandably insisted on closer acquaintance, he would return his dispatches to headquarters at Z— for delivery by someone else, and accept their kind offer of hospitality in this house for a few weeks. So saying he paused for a moment, standing by the wall with his chair in his hand, and looked at the Commandant. The latter replied that he would be extremely sorry if the Count were to get himself into possibly very serious trouble as a result of the passion which he seemed to have conceived for his daughter; that he himself, however, presumably knew best what his duties were; that he should therefore send off his dispatches and move into the rooms which were at his disposal. The Count was seen to change colour on hearing this; he then kissed his hostess's hand respectfully, bowed to the others, and withdrew.

When he had left the room, the family was at a loss to know what to make of this scene. The Marquise's mother said she could hardly believe it possible that having set out

14

for Naples with dispatches he would send them back to Z— merely because on his way through M— he had failed, in a conversation lasting five minutes, to extract a promise of marriage from a lady with whom he was totally unacquainted. Her son pointed out that for such frivolous behaviour he would at the very least be arrested and confined to barracks. 'And cashiered as well!' added the Commandant. But, he went on, there was in fact no such danger. The Count had merely been firing a warning salvo, and would surely think again before actually sending back the dispatches. His wife, hearing of the danger to which the young man would be exposing himself by sending them off, expressed the liveliest anxiety that he might in fact do so. She thought that his headstrong nature, obstinately bent on one single purpose, would be capable of precisely such an act. She most urgently entreated her son to go after the Count at once and dissuade him from so fatal a step. Her son replied that if he did so it would have exactly the opposite effect, and merely confirm the Count's hopes of winning the day by his intended stratagem. The Marquise was of the same opinion, though she predicted that if her brother did not take this action it was quite certain that the dispatches would be returned, since the Count would prefer to risk the consequences rather than expose his honour to any aspersion. All were agreed that his behaviour was extraordinary, and that he seemed to be accustomed to taking ladies' hearts, like fortresses, by storm. At this point the Commandant noticed that the Count's carriage was standing by his front door with the horses harnessed and ready. He called his family to the window to look, and asked one of the servants who now entered whether the Count was still in the house. The servant replied that he was downstairs in the servants' quarters, attended by an adjutant, writing letters and sealing up packages. The Commandant, concealing his dismay, hurried downstairs with his son and, seeing the Count busy at work on a table that did not well befit him, asked whether he would not rather make use of his own apartments, and whether there was not anything else they could do to meet his requirements. The Count, continuing to write with great rapidity, replied that he was deeply obliged, but that he had now finished his business; as he sealed the letter he also asked what time it was; he then handed over the entire portfolio to the adjutant and wished him a safe journey. The Commandant, scarcely believing his eyes, said as the adjutant left the house: 'Count, unless your reasons are extremely weighty—' 'They are absolutely compelling!' said the Count, interrupting him. He accompanied the adjutant to the carriage and opened the door for him. The Commandant persisted: 'In that case I would at least send the dispatches—' 'Impossible!' answered the Count, helping the adjutant into his seat. 'The dispatches would carry no authority in Naples without me. I did think of that too. Drive on!' 'And your uncle's letters, sir?' called the adjutant, leaning out of the carriage door. 'They will reach me in M—,' replied the Count. 'Drive on!' said the adjutant, and the carriage sped on its way.

Count F— then turned to the Commandant and asked him

if he would be kind enough to have him shown to his room. 'It will be an honour for me to show you to it at once,' answered the bewildered Colonel. He called to his servants and to the Count's servants, telling them to look after the latter's luggage; he then conducted him to the apartments in his house which were set aside for guests and there rather stiffly took his leave of him. The Count changed his clothes, left the house to report his presence to the military governor, and was not seen in the house for the whole of the rest of that day, only returning just before dinner.

In the meantime the family were in considerable dismay. The Commandant's son described how categorical the Count's replies had been when his father had attempted to reason with him; his action, he thought, was to all appearances deliberate and considered; what on earth, he wondered, could be the motive of this post-haste wooing? The Commandant said that the whole thing was beyond his comprehension, and forbade the family to mention the subject again in his presence. His wife kept on looking out of the window as if she expected the Count to return, express regret for his hasty action, and take steps to reverse it. Eventually, when it grew dark, she joined her daughter who was sitting at a table absorbed in some work and evidently intent on avoiding conversation. As the Commandant paced up and down, she asked her in an undertone whether she had any idea of how this matter would end. The Marquise, with a diffident glance towards the Commandant, replied that if only her father could have prevailed on him to go to Naples, everything would have been all right. 'To Naples!' exclaimed her father, who had overheard his remark. 'Ought I to have sent for a priest? Or should I have had him arrested, locked up and sent to Naples under guard?' 'No,' answered his daughter, 'but emphatic remonstrances can be effective.' And she rather crossly looked down at her work again. Finally, towards nightfall, the Count reappeared. The family fully expected that, after the first exchange of courtesies, discussion of the point in question would be reopened, and they would then join in unanimously imploring him to retract, if it were still possible, the bold step he had taken. But a suitable moment for this exhortation was awaited in vain throughout dinner. Sedulously avoiding anything that might have led on to that particular topic, he conversed with the Commandant about the war and with his son, the forester, about hunting. When he mentioned the engagement at P— in the course of which he had been wounded, the Marquise's mother elicited from him an account of his illness, asking him how he had fared at so tiny a place and whether he had been provided there with all proper comforts. In answer he told them various interesting details relevant to his passion for the Marquise: how during his illness she had been constantly present to him, sitting at his bedside; how in the feverish delirium brought on by his wound he had kept confusing his visions of her with the sight of a swan, which, as a boy, he had watched on his uncle's estate; that he had been particularly moved by one memory, of an occasion on which he had once thrown some mud at this swan, whereupon it had silently dived under the surface and re-emerged, washed clean by the water; that she had always seemed to be swimming about on a fiery surface and that he had called out to her 'Tinka!', which had been the swan's name, but that he had not been able to lure her towards him. For she had preferred merely to glide about, arching her neck and thrusting out her breast. Suddenly, blushing scarlet, he declared that he loved her more than he could say; then looked down again at his plate and fell silent. At last it was time to rise from the table; and when the Count, after a further brief conversation with the Marquise's mother, bowed to the company and retired again to his room, they were all once more left standing there not knowing what to think. The Commandant was of the opinion that they must simply let things take their course. The Count, in acting as he did, was no doubt relying on his relatives without whose intervention on his behalf he must certainly face dishonourable discharge. The Marquise's mother asked her what she felt about him, and whether she could not perhaps bring herself to give him some indication or other that might avert an unfortunate outcome. Her daughter replied: 'My dear mother, that is impossible! I am sorry that my gratitude is being put to so severe a test. But I did decide not to marry again; I do not like to chance my happiness a second time, and certainly not with such ill-considered haste.' Her brother observed that if such was her firm intention, then a declaration to *that* effect could also help the Count, and that it looked rather as if they would have to give him *some* definite answer, one way or the other. The Colonel's wife replied that since the young man had so many outstanding qualities to recommend him, and had declared himself ready to settle in Italy, she thought that his offer deserved some consideration and that the Marquise should reflect carefully before deciding. Her son, sitting down beside his sister, asked her whether she found the Count personally attractive. The Marquise, with some embarrassment, answered that she found him both attractive and unattractive, and that she was willing to be guided by what the others felt. Her mother said: 'When he comes back from Naples, and if between now and then we were to make inquiries which did not reveal anything that ran contrary to the general impression you have formed of him, then what answer would you give him if he were to repeat his proposal?' 'In that case,' replied the Marquise, 'I—since his wishes do seem to be so pressing'—she faltered at this point and her eyes shone—'I would consent to them for the sake of the obligation under which he has placed me.' Her mother, who had always hoped that her daughter would re-marry, had difficulty in concealing her delight at this declaration, and sat considering to what advantage it might be turned. Her son, getting up again in some uneasiness, said that if the Marquise were even remotely considering a possibility of one day bestowing her hand in marriage on the Count, some step in this direction must now immediately be taken if the consequences of his reckless course of action were to be forestalled. His mother agreed, remarking that after all they could be taking no very great risk, since the young man had displayed so many excellent qualities on the night of the Russian assault on the fortress that there was every reason to assume him to be a person of consistently good character. The Marquise cast down her eyes with an air of considerable agitation. 'After all,' continued her mother, taking her by the hand, 'one could perhaps intimate to him that until he returns from Naples you undertake not to enter into any other engagement.' The Marquise said: 'Dearest mother, *that* undertaking I can give him; but I fear it will not satisfy him and only compromise us.' 'Let me take care of that!' replied her mother, much elated; she looked round for her husband and seemed about to rise to her feet. 'Lorenzo!' she asked, 'What do you think?' The Commandant, who had heard this whole discussion, went on standing by the window, looking down into the street, and said nothing. The Marquise's brother declared that, on the strength of this noncommittal assurance from her, he would now personally guarantee to get the Count out of the house. 'Well then, do so! do so! Do so, all of you!' exclaimed his father, turning round. 'That makes twice already I must surrender to this Russian!' At this his wife sprang to her feet, kissed him and their daughter, and asked, with an eagerness which made her husband smile, how they were to set about conveying this intimation without delay to the Count. At her son's suggestion it was decided to send a footman to his room requesting him to be so kind, if he were not already undressed, as to rejoin the family for a moment. The Count sent back word that he would at once have the honour to appear, and scarcely had this message been brought when he himself, joy winging his step, followed it into the room and sank to his knees, with deep emotion, at the Marquise's feet. The Commandant was about to speak, but Count F—, standing up, declared that he already knew enough. He kissed the Colonel's hand and that of his wife, embraced the Marquise's brother, and merely asked if they would do him the favour of helping him to find a coach immediately. The Marquise, though visibly touched by this scene, nevertheless managed to say: 'I need not fear, Count, that rash hopes will mislead—' 'By no means, by no means!' replied the Count. 'I will hold you to nothing, if the outcome of such inquiries as you may make about me is in any way adverse to the feeling which has just recalled me to your presence.' At this the Commandant heartily embraced him, the Marquise's brother at once offered him his own travelling-carriage, a groom was dispatched in haste to the post-station to order horses at a premium rate, and there was more pleasure at this departure than has ever been shown at a guest's arrival. The Count said that he hoped to overtake his dispatches in B—, whence he now proposed to set out for Naples by a shorter route than the one through M—; in Naples he would do his utmost to get himself released from the further mission to Constantinople; in the last resort he was resolved to report himself as sick, and could therefore assure them that unless prevented by unavoidable circumstances he would without fail be back in M— within four to six weeks. At this point his groom reported that the carriage was harnessed and everything ready for his departure. The Count picked up his hat, went up to the Marquise and took her hand. 'Well, Giulietta,' he said, 'this sets my mind partly at rest.' Laying his hand in hers he added, 'Yet it was my dearest wish that before I left we should be married.' 'Married!' exclaimed the whole family. 'Married,' repeated the Count, kissing the Marquise's hand, and when she asked him whether he had taken leave of his senses he assured her that a day would come when she would understand what he meant. The family was on the point of losing patience with him, but he at once most warmly took his leave of them all, asked them to take no further notice of his last remark, and departed.

Several weeks passed, during which the family, with very mixed feelings, awaited the outcome of this strange affair. The Commandant received a courteous letter from General K—, the Count's uncle; the Count himself wrote from Naples; inquiries about him were put in hand and quite favourable reports received; in brief, the engagement was already regarded as virtually definitive—when the Marquise's indispositions recurred, more acutely than ever before. She noticed an incomprehensible change in her figure. She confided with complete frankness in her mother, telling her that she did not know what to make of her condition. Her mother, learning of these strange symptoms, became extremely concerned about her daughter's health and insisted that she should consult a doctor. The Marquise, hoping that her natural good health would reassert itself, resisted this advice; she suffered severely for several more days without following it, until constantly repeated sensations of the most unusual kind threw her into a state of acute anxiety. She sent for a doctor who enjoyed the confidence of her father; at a time when her mother happened to be out of the house she invited him to sit down on the divan, and after an introductory remark or two jestingly told him what condition she believed herself to be in. The doctor gave her a searching look; he then carefully examined her, and after doing so was silent for a little; finally he answered with a very grave expression that the Marquise had judged correctly how things were. When the lady inquired what exactly he meant he explained himself unequivocally, adding with a smile which he could not suppress that she was perfectly well and needed no doctor, whereupon the Marquise rang the bell and with a very severe sidelong glance requested him to leave her. She murmured to herself in an undertone, as if it were beneath her dignity to address him, that she did not feel inclined to joke with him about such matters. The doctor, offended, replied that he could only wish she had always been as much in earnest as she was now; so saying, he picked up his hat and stick and made as if to take his leave. The Marquise assured him that she would inform her father of his insulting remarks. The doctor answered that he would swear to his statement in any court of law; with that he opened the door, bowed, and was about to leave the room. As he paused to pick up a glove he had dropped, the Marquise exclaimed: 'But doctor, how is what you say possible?' The doctor replied that she would presumably not expect him to explain the facts of life to her; he then bowed again and withdrew.

The Marquise stood as if thunderstruck. Recovering herself, she was on the point of going straight to her father; but the strangely serious manner of this man by whom she felt so insulted numbed her in every limb. She threw herself down on the divan in the greatest agitation. Mistrustful of herself, she cast her mind back over every moment of the past year, and when she thought of those through which she had just passed it seemed to her that she must be going crazy. At last her mother appeared, and in answer to her shocked inquiry as to why she was so distressed, the Marquise informed her of what the doctor had just said. Her mother declared him to be a shameless and contemptible wretch, and emboldened her in her resolution to report his insult to her father. The Marquise assured her that the doctor had been completely in earnest and seemed quite determined to repeat his insane assertion to her father's face. Did she then, asked her mother in some alarm, believe there was any possibility of her being in such a condition? 'I would sooner believe that graves can be made fertile,' answered the Marquise, 'and that new births can quicken in the womb of the dead!' 'Why then, you dear strange girl,' said her mother, hugging her warmly, 'what can be worrying you? If your conscience clears you, what can a doctor's verdict matter, or indeed the verdict of a whole panel of doctors? This particular one may be mistaken, or he may be malicious, but why need that concern you at all? Nevertheless it is proper that we should tell your father about it.' 'Oh, God!' said the Marquise, starting convulsively, 'how can I set my mind at rest? Do not my own feelings speak against me, those inner sensations I know only too well? If I knew that another woman was feeling as I do, would I not myself come to the conclusion that that was indeed how things stood with her?' 'But this is terrible!' exclaimed her mother. 'Malicious! mistaken!' continued the Marquise. 'What reasons can that man, whom until today we have always respected, what reasons can he have for insulting me so frivolously and basely? Why should he do so, when I have never said anything to offend him? When I received him here with complete trust, fully expecting to be bound to him in gratitude? When he came to me sincerely and honestly intending, as was evident from his very first words, to help me rather than to cause me far worse pain than I was already suffering? And if on the other hand,' she went on, while her mother gazed at her steadily, 'I were forced to choose between the two possibilities and preferred to suppose that he had made a mistake, is it in the least possible that a doctor, even one of quite mediocre skill, should be mistaken in such a case?' Her mother replied, a little ironically: 'And yet, of course, it must necessarily have been one or the other.' 'Yes, dearest mother!' answered the Marquise, kissing her hand but with an air of offended dignity and blushing scarlet, 'it must indeed, although the circumstances are so extraordinary that I may be permitted to doubt it. And since it seems that I must give you an assurance, I swear now that my conscience is as clear as that of my own children's; no less clear, my beloved and respected mother, than your own. Nevertheless, I ask you to have a midwife called in to see me, in order

26

that I may convince myself of what is the case and then, whatever it may be, set my mind at rest.' 'A midwife!' exclaimed the Commandant's wife indignantly, 'a clear conscience, and a midwife!' And speech failed her. 'A midwife, my dearest mother,' repeated the Marquise, falling on her knees before her, 'and let her come at once, if I am not to go out of my mind.' 'Oh, by all means,' replied her mother. 'But the confinement, if you please, will not take place in my house.' And with these words she rose and would have left the room. Her daughter, following her with outspread arms, fell right down on her face and clasped her knees. 'If the irreproachable life I have led,' she cried, with anguish lending her eloquence, 'a life modelled on yours, gives me any claim at all to your respect, if there is in your heart any maternal feeling for me at all, even if only for so long as my guilt is not yet proved and clear as day, then do not abandon me at this terrible moment!' 'But what is upsetting you?' asked her mother. 'Is it nothing more than the doctor's verdict? Nothing more than your inner sensations?' 'Nothing more, dear mother,' replied the Marquise, laying her hand on her breast. 'Nothing, Giulietta?' continued her mother. 'Think carefully. If you have committed a fault, though that would grieve me indescribably, it would be forgivable and in the end I should have to forgive it; but if, in order to avoid censure from your mother, you were to invent a fable about the overturning of the whole order of nature, and dared to reiterate blasphemous vows in order to persuade me of its truth, knowing that my heart is all too eager to believe you, then that would

27

be shameful; I could never feel the same about you again.' 'May the doors of salvation one day be as open to me as my soul is now open to you!' cried the Marquise. 'I have concealed nothing from you, mother.' This declaration, uttered with passionate solemnity, moved her mother deeply. 'Oh, God!' she cried, 'my dear, dear child! How touchingly you speak!' And she lifted her up and kissed her and pressed her to her heart. 'Then what in the name of all the world are you afraid of? Come, you are quite ill,' she added, trying to lead her towards a bed. But the Marquise, weeping copiously, assured her that she was quite well and that there was nothing wrong with her, apart from her extraordinary and incomprehensible condition. 'Condition!' exclaimed her mother again, 'what condition? If your recollection of the past is so clear, what mad apprehension has possessed you? Can one not be deceived by such internal sensations, when they are still only obscurely stirring?' 'No! no!' said the Marquise, 'they are not deceiving me! And if you will have the midwife called, then you will hear that this terrible, annihilating thing is true.' 'Come, my darling,' said the Commandant's wife, who was beginning to fear for her daughter's reason. 'Come with me; you must go to bed. What was it you thought the doctor said to you? Why, your cheeks are burning hot! You're trembling in every limb! Now, what was it the doctor told you?' And no longer believing that the scene of which she had been told had really happened at all, she took her daughter by the arm and tried to draw her away. Then the Marquise, smiling through her tears, said: 'My dear, excellent mother! I am in full possession of my senses. The doctor told me that I am expecting a child. Send for the midwife; and as soon as she tells me that it is not true I shall regain my composure.' 'Very well, very well!' replied her mother, concealing her apprehension. 'She shall come at once; if that is what you want, she shall come and laugh her head off at you and tell you what a silly girl you are to imagine such things.' And so saying she rang the bell and immediately sent one of her servants to call the midwife.

When the latter arrived the Marquise was still lying with her mother's arms around her and her breast heaving in agitation. The Commandant's wife told the woman of the strange notion by which her daughter was afflicted: that her ladyship swore her behaviour had been entirely virtuous but that nevertheless, deluded by some mysterious sensation or other, she considered it necessary to submit her condition to the scrutiny of a woman with professional knowledge. The midwife, as she carried out her investigation, spoke of warm-blooded youth and the wiles of the world; having finished her task she remarked that she had come across such cases before; young widows who found themselves in her ladyship's situation always believed themselves to have been living on desert islands; but that there was no cause for alarm, and her ladyship could rest assured that the gay corsair who had come ashore in the dark would come to light in due course. On hearing these words, the Marquise fainted. Her mother was still sufficiently moved by natural affection to bring her back to her senses with the midwife's assistance, but as soon as she revived, maternal indignation proved stronger. 'Giulietta!' she cried in anguish, 'will you confess to me, will you tell me who the father is?' And she still seemed disposed towards a reconciliation. But when the Marquise replied that she would go mad, her mother rose from the couch and said: 'Go from my sight, you are contemptible! I curse the day I bore you!' and left the room.

The Marquise, now nearly swooning again, drew the midwife down in front of her and laid her head against her breast, trembling violently. With a faltering voice she asked her what the ways of nature were, and whether such a thing as an unwitting conception was possible. The woman smiled, loosened her kerchief and said that that would, she was sure, not be the case with her ladyship. 'No, no,' answered the Marquise, 'I conceived knowingly, I am merely curious in a general way whether such a phenomenon exists in the realm of nature.' The midwife replied that with the exception of the Blessed Virgin it had never yet happened to any woman on earth. The Marquise trembled more violently than ever. She felt as if she might go into labour at any minute, and clung to the midwife in convulsive fear, begging her not to leave her. The woman calmed her apprehension, assuring her that the confinement was still a long way off; she also informed her of the ways and means by which it was possible in such cases to avoid the gossip of the world, and said she was sure everything would turn out nicely. But these consoling remarks merely pierced the unhappy lady to the very heart;

composing herself with an effort she declared that she felt better, and requested her attendant to leave her.

The midwife was scarcely out of the room when a footman brought the Marquise a written message from her mother, who expressed herself as follows: 'In view of the circumstances which have come to light, Colonel G— desires you to leave his house. He sends you herewith the papers concerning your estate and hopes that God will spare him the unhappiness of ever seeing you again.' But the letter was wet with tears, and in one corner, half effaced, stood the word 'dictated'. Tears of grief started from the Marquise's eyes. Weeping bitterly at the thought of the error into which her excellent parents had fallen and the injustice into which it had misled them, she went to her mother's apartments, but was told that her mother was with the Commandant. Hardly able to walk, she made her way to her father's rooms. Finding the door locked she sank down outside it, and in a heart-rending voice called upon all the saints to witness her innocence. She had been lying there for perhaps a few minutes when her brother emerged, his face flushed with anger, and said that as she already knew, the Commandant did not wish to see her. The Marquise, sobbing distractedly, exclaimed: 'Dearest brother!', and pushing her way into the room she cried: 'My beloved father!' She held out her arms towards the Commandant, but no sooner did he see her than he turned his back on her and hurried into his bedroom. As she tried to follow him he shouted 'Begone!' and tried to slam the door; but when she cried out imploringly and prevented him from doing so he suddenly desisted and letting the Marquise into the room, strode across to the far side of it with his back still turned to her. She had just thrown herself at his feet and tremblingly clasped his knees when a pistol which he had seized went off just as he was snatching it down from the wall, and a shot crashed into the ceiling. 'Oh, God preserve me!' exclaimed the Marquise, rising from her knees as pale as death, and fled from her father's apartment. Reaching her own, she gave orders that her carriage should be made ready at once, sat down in utter exhaustion, hastily dressed her children, and told the servants to pack her belongings. She was just holding her youngest child between her knees, wrapping one more garment round it, and everything was ready for their departure in the carriage, when her brother entered and demanded, on the Commandant's orders that she should leave the children behind and hand them over to him. 'These children!' she exclaimed, rising to her feet. 'Tell your inhuman father that he can come here and shoot me dead, but he shall not take my children from me!' And armed with all the pride of innocence she snatched up her children, carried them with her to the coach, her brother not daring to stop her, and drove off.

This splendid effort of will gave her back her self-confidence, and as if with her own hands she raised herself right out of the depths into which fate had cast her. The turmoil and anguish of her heart ceased when she found herself on the open road with her beloved prize, the children; she covered them with kisses, reflecting with great satisfaction what a victory she had won over her brother by the sheer force of her clear conscience. Her reason was strong enough to withstand her strange situation without giving way, and she submitted herself wholly to the great, sacred and inexplicable order of the world. She saw that it would be impossible to convince her family of her innocence, realized that she must accept this fact for the sake of her own survival, and only a few days after her arrival at V— her grief had been replaced by a heroic resolve to arm herself with pride and let the world do its worst. She decided to withdraw altogether into her own life, to devote herself zealously and exclusively to the education of her two children, and to care with full maternal love for the third which God had now given her. Since her beautiful country house had fallen rather into disrepair owing to her long absence, she made arrangements for its restoration, to be completed in a few weeks' time, as soon as her confinement was over; she sat in the summer-house knitting little caps and socks for little feet, and thinking about what use she might most conveniently make of various rooms, which of them for instance she would fill with books and in which of them her easel might be most suitably placed. And thus, even before the date of Count F—'s expected return from Naples, she was quite reconciled to a life of perpetual cloistered seclusion. Her porter was ordered to admit no visitors to the house. The only thing she found intolerable was the thought that the little creature she had conceived in the utmost innocence and purity and whose origin, precisely because it was more mysterious, also seemed to her

33

more divine than that of other men, was destined to bear a stigma of disgrace in good society. An unusual expedient for discovering the father had occurred to her: an expedient which, when she first thought of it, so startled her that she let fall her knitting. For whole nights on end, restless and sleepless, she turned it over and over in her mind, trying to get used to an idea the very nature of which offended her innermost feelings. She still felt the greatest repugnance at the thought of entering into any relationship with the person who had tricked her in such a fashion; for she most rightly concluded that he must after all irredeemably belong to the very scum of mankind, and that whatever position of society one might imagine him to occupy, his origin could only be from its lowest, vilest dregs. But with her sense of her own independence growing ever stronger, and reflecting as she did that a precious stone retains its value whatever its setting may be, she took heart one morning, as she felt the stirring of the new life inside her, and gave instructions for the insertion in the M— news-sheets of the extraordinary announcement quoted to the reader at the beginning of this story.

Meanwhile Count F—, detained in Naples by unavoidable duties, had written for the second time to the Marquise urging her to consider that unusual circumstances might arise which would make it desirable for her to abide by the tacit undertaking she had given him. As soon as he had succeeded in declining his further official journey to Constantinople, and as soon as his other business permitted, he at once left Naples and duly arrived in M—only a few days later than the date on which he had said he would do so. The Commandant received him with an air of embarrassment, said that he was about to leave the house on urgent business, and asked his son to entertain the Count in the meantime. The latter took him to his room and, after greeting him briefly, asked him whether he already knew about what had happened in the Commandant's house during his absence. The Count, turning pale for a moment, answered that he did not. The Marquise's brother thereupon informed him of the disgrace which his sister had brought upon the family, and narrated the events with which our readers are already acquainted. The Count struck his forehead with his hand and exclaimed, quite forgetting himself: 'Why were so many obstacles put in my way! If the marriage had taken place, we should have been spared all this shame and unhappiness!' The Commandant's son, staring at him wide-eyed, asked him whether he was so crazy as to want to be married to so contemptible a person. The Count replied that she was worth more than the whole of the world which despised her; that he for his part absolutely believed her declaration of innocence; and that he would go that very day to V— and renew his offer to her. So saying he at once picked up his hat and left, after bidding farewell to the Commandant's son, who concluded that he must have taken leave of his senses.

Taking a horse he galloped out to V—. When he had dismounted at the gate and was about to enter the forecourt, the porter told him that her ladyship was not at home to anyone. The Count inquired whether these instructions, issued presumably to keep away strangers, also applied to a friend of the family, to which the man answered that he was not aware of any exceptions to them; and he then almost at once inquired, in a rather dubious manner, whether the gentleman were not perhaps Count F—? The Count, after glancing at him sharply, answered that he was not; then turning to his servant, but speaking loudly enough for the other man to hear, he said that in these circumstances he would lodge at an inn and announce himself to her ladyship in writing. But as soon as he was out of the porter's sight he turned a corner and slipped quietly round the wall of an extensive garden which lay behind the house. By a door which he found unlocked he entered the garden, walked through it along the paths, and was just about to ascend the terrace to the rear of the house when in an arbour at one side of it he caught sight of the Marquise, her figure charmingly and mysteriously altered, sitting busily working at a little table. He approached her in such a manner that she could not notice him until he was standing at the entrance to the arbour, three short steps from her feet. 'Count F—!" she exclaimed as she looked up, blushing scarlet with surprise. The Count smiled, and remained standing motionless in the entrance for some moments; then, with a show of affection sufficiently modest not to alarm her, he sat down at her side, and before she could make up her mind what to do in so strange a situation, he put his arm gently and lovingly around her waist. 'But Count, how is this possible, where have you—' began the Marquise, and then shyly cast down her eyes. 'From M—,' said the Count, pressing her very gently to him. 'I found a back door open and came through it into your garden; I felt sure you would forgive me for doing so.' 'But when you were in M— did they not tell you—?' she asked, still motionless in his arms. 'Everything, dearest lady,' replied the Count. 'But fully convinced of your innocence—' 'What!' cried the Marquise, rising to her feet and trying to free herself from him, 'and despite that you come here?' 'Despite the world,' he went on, holding her fast, 'and despite your family, and even despite your present enchanting appearance'—at which words he ardently kissed her breast. 'Go away!' she exclaimed, but he continued: '—as convinced, Giulietta, as if I were omniscient, as if my own soul were living in your body.' The Marquise cried: 'Let me go!' 'I have come,' he concluded, still without releasing her, 'to repeat my proposal and to receive, if you will accept it, the bliss of paradise from your hand.' 'Let me go immediately!' she cried, 'I order you to let me go!', and freeing herself forcibly from his embrace she stared away from him. 'Darling! adorable creature!' he whispered, rising to his feet again and following her. 'You heard me!' cried the Marquise, turning and evading him. 'One secret, whispered word!' said the Count, hastily snatching at her smooth arm as it slipped from him. 'I *do not want to hear* anything,' she retorted, violently pushing him back; then she fled up on to the terrace and disappeared.

He was already half-way up to her, determined at all costs to get a hearing, when the door was slammed in his face, and in front of his hurrying steps he heard the bolt rattle as with distraught vehemence she pushed it home. He stood for a moment undecided what to do in this situation, considering whether he should climb in through a side window which was standing open, and pursue his purpose until he had achieved it; but although it was in every sense difficult for him to desist, it did now seem necessary to do so, and bitterly vexed with himself for letting her slip from his arms, he retreated from the terrace, left the garden, and went to find his horse. He felt that his attempt to pour out his heart to her in person had failed forever, and rode slowly back to M—, thinking over the wording of a letter which he now felt condemned to write. That evening, as he was dining in a public place, very much out of humour, he met the Marquise's brother, who at once asked him whether he had successfully made his proposal in V—. The Count answered curtly that he had not, and felt very much inclined to dismiss his interlocutor with some bitter phrase; but for the sake of politeness he presently added that he had decided to write the lady a letter, which would soon clarify the issue. The Commandant's son said he noticed with regret that the Count's passion for his sister was driving him quite out of his mind. He must, however, assure the Count that she was already on her way to making a different choice; so saying he rang for the latest newspapers and gave the Count the sheet in which was inserted his sister's advertisement appealing to the father of her child. The Count flushed suddenly as he read it; conflicting emotions rushed through him. The Marquise's brother asked him if he did not think that she would find the person she was looking for. 'Undoubtedly!' answered the Count, with his whole mind intent on the paper, greedily devouring the meaning of the announcement. Then, after folding it up and stepping over to the window for a moment, he said: 'Now everything is all right! Now I know what to do!' He then turned round, and after courteously asking the Commandant's son whether they would soon meet again, he took his leave of him and departed, quite reconciled to his lot.

Meanwhile some very animated scenes had taken place at the Commandant's house. His wife was in a state of extreme vexation at her husband's destructive vehemence and at her own weakness in allowing him to overrule her objections to his tyrannical banishment of their daughter. When she heard the pistol shot in his bedroom and saw her daughter rushing out of it she had fainted away; she had, to be sure, soon recovered herself, but all the Commandant did when she came to her senses was to apologize for causing her this unnecessary alarm, and throw the discharged pistol down on to a table. Later, when it was proposed to claim custody of their daughter's children, she timorously ventured to declare that they had no right to take such a step; in a voice still weak from her recent swoon, she touchingly implored him to avoid violent scenes in the house; but the Commandant, not answering her, had merely turned foaming with rage to his son and ordered him: 'Go to her! and bring them back here!' When Count F—'s second letter arrived, the Commandant had ordered that it should be sent out to the Marquise at V—; the messenger afterwards reported that she had simply laid it on one side and dismissed him. Her mother, to whom so much in this whole affair was incomprehensible, more particularly her daughter's inclination to get married again and to someone totally indifferent to her, tried vainly to initiate a discussion of this point. Each time she did so the Commandant requested her to be silent, in a manner more like an order than a request; on one such occasion he removed from the wall a portrait of his daughter that was still hanging there, declaring that he wished to expunge her completely from his memory; he no longer, he said, had a daughter. Then the Marquise's strange advertisement was published. The Commandant had handed the paper containing it to his wife, who read it with absolute amazement and went with it to her husband's rooms, where she found him working at a table, and asking him what on earth he thought of it. The Commandant continuing to write, said: 'Oh, she is innocent!' 'What!' exclaimed his wife, astonished beyond measure, 'innocent?' 'She did it in her sleep,' said the Commandant, without looking up. 'In her sleep!' replied his wife. 'And you are telling me that such a monstrous occurrence—' 'Silly woman!' exclaimed the Commandant, pushing his papers together and leaving the room.

On the next day on which news was published the Commandant's wife, seated with her husband at breakfast, was handed a news-sheet which had just arrived not yet dry from the printers, and in it she read the following answer: 'If the Marquise of O— will be present at 11 o'clock on the morning of the 3rd of — in the house of her father Colonel G—, the man whom she wishes to trace will there cast himself at her feet.'

The Colonel's wife became speechless before she had even read halfway through this extraordinary insertion; she glanced at the end, and handed the sheet to the Commandant. The latter read it through three times, as if he could not believe his own eyes. 'Now tell me, in heaven's name, Lorenzo,' cried his wife, 'what do you make of that?' 'Why, the infamous woman!' replied the Commandant, rising from the table, 'the sanctimonious hypocrite! The shamelessness of a bitch coupled with the cunning of a fox and multiplied tenfold are as nothing to hers! So sweet a face! Such eyes, as innocent as a cherub!' And nothing could calm his distress. 'But if it is a trick,' asked his wife, 'what on earth can be her purpose!' 'Her purpose?' retorted the Colonel. 'She is determined to force us to accept her contemptible pretence. She and that man have already learnt by heart the cock-and-bull story they will tell us when the two of them appear here on the third at eleven in the morning. And I shall be expected to say: "My dear little daughter, I did not know that, who could have thought such a thing, forgive me, receive my blessing, and let us be friends again." But I have a bullet ready for the man who steps across my threshold on the third! Or perhaps it would be more suitable to have him thrown out of the house by the servants.' His wife, after a further perusal of the announcement in the paper, said that if she was to believe one of two incomprehensible things, then she found it more credible that some extraordinary quirk of fate had occurred than that a daughter who had always been so virtuous should now behave so basely. But before she had even finished speaking, her husband was already shouting: 'Be so good as to hold your tongue! I cannot bear,' he added, leaving the room, 'even to hear this hateful matter mentioned.'

A few days later the Commandant received a letter from the Marquise referring to the second announcement, and most respectfully and touchingly begging him, since she had been deprived of the privilege of setting foot in his house, to be so kind as to send whoever presented himself there on the morning of the third out to her estate at V—. Her mother happened to be present when the Commandant received this letter, and she noticed by the expression on his face that his feelings had become confused; for if the whole thing was indeed a trick, what motive was he to impute to her now, since she seemed to be making no sort of claim to his forgiveness? Emboldened by this, she accordingly proposed a plan which her heart, troubled by doubts as it was, had for some time been harbouring. As her husband still stared expressionlessly at the paper, she said that she had an idea. Would he allow her to go for one or two days out to V—? She undertook to devise a situation in which the Marquise, if she really knew the man who had answered her advertisement as if he were a stranger, would undoubtedly betray herself, even if she was the world's most sophisticated deceiver. The Commandant, with sudden violence, tore his daughter's letter to shreds, and replied to his wife that, as she well knew, he wished to have nothing whatever to do with its writer, and absolutely forbade her mother to enter into any communication with her. He sealed up the torn pieces in an envelope, wrote the Marquise's address on it, and returned it to the messenger as his answer. His wife, inwardly exasperated by this headstrong obstinacy which would destroy any possibility they had of clearing the matter up, now decided to carry out her plan against her husband's will. On the very next morning, while the Commandant was still in bed, she took one of his grooms and drove with him out to V——. When she reached the gate of her daughter's country house, the porter told her that his orders were to admit no one to her ladyship's presence. The Commandant's wife replied that she knew of these orders, but that he was nevertheless to go and announce the wife of Colonel G——. To this the man answered that it would be useless to do so, since his mistress was receiving no one, and there were no exceptions. The Commandant's wife answered that she would be received by his mistress, as she was her mother; would he therefore be good enough to do his errand without further delay. But scarcely had the man, still predicting that this mission would be fruitless, entered the house than the Marquise was seen to emerge from it and come in haste to the gate, where she fell on her knees before her mother's carriage. The latter, assisted by her groom, stepped down from it, and in some emotion raised her daughter from the ground. The Marquise, quite overwhelmed by her feelings, bowed low over her mother's hand to kiss it; then, shedding frequent tears, she very respectfully conducted her through the rooms of her house and seated her on a divan.

'My dearest mother!' she exclaimed, still standing in front of her and drying her eyes, 'to what happy chance do I owe the inexpressible pleasure of your visit?' Her mother, taking her affectionately by the hand, said that she must tell her she had simply come to ask her forgiveness for the hard-hearted way in which she had been expelled from her parents' house. 'Forgiveness!' cried the Marquise, and tried to kiss her hand. But her mother, withdrawing her hand, continued: 'For not only did the recently published answer to—your advertisement convince myself and your father of your innocence, but I have also to tell you that the man in question, to our great delight and surprise, has already presented himself at our house yesterday.' '*Who* has already—?' asked the Marquise, sitting down beside her mother, '*what* man in question has presented himself—?' And her face was tense with expectation. Her mother answered: 'The man who wrote that reply, he himself in person, the man to whom your appeal was directed.' 'Well, then,' said the Marquise, with her breast heaving in agitation, 'who is he?' And she repeated: 'Who is he?' 'That,' replied her mother, 'is what I should like you to guess. For just imagine: yesterday, as we were sitting at tea, and in the act of reading that extraordinary newspaper announcement, a man with whom we are quite intimately acquainted rushed into the room with gestures of despair and threw himself down at your father's feet, and presently at mine as well. We had no idea what to make of this and asked him to explain himself. So he said that his conscience was giving him no peace, it was he who had so shamefully deceived our daughter; he could not but know how his crime was judged, and if retribution was to be exacted from him for it, he had come to submit himself to that retribution.' 'But who? who? who?' asked the Marquise. 'As I told you,' continued her mother, 'an otherwise well-brought-up young man whom we should never have considered capable of so base an act. But my dear daughter, you must not be alarmed to hear that he is of humble station, and quite lacks all the qualifications that a husband of yours might otherwise be expected to have.' 'Nevertheless, my most excellent mother,' said the Marquise, 'he cannot be wholly unworthy, since he came and threw himself at your feet before throwing himself at mine. But who? who? please tell me *who*!' 'Well,' replied her mother, 'it was Leopardo, the groom from Tyrol whom your father recently engaged, and whom as you may have noticed I have already brought with me to present to you as your fiancé.' 'Leopardo, the groom!' cried the Marquise, pressing her hand to her forehead with an expression of despair. 'Why are you startled?' asked her mother. 'Have you reasons for doubting it?' 'How? where? when?' asked the Marquise in confusion. 'That,' answered her mother, 'is something he wishes to confess only to you. Shame and love, he told us, made it impossible for him to communicate these facts to anyone except yourself. But if you like we will open the anteroom, where he is waiting with a beating heart for the outcome, and then I shall leave you together, and you will see whether you can elicit his secret from him.' 'Oh, God in heaven!' cried the Marquise: 'it did once happen that I had fallen asleep in the mid-day heat, on my divan, and when I woke up I saw him walking away from it!' Her face grew scarlet with shame and she covered it with her little hands. But at this point her mother fell to her knees before her. 'Oh, Giulietta!' she exclaimed, throwing her arms round her, 'oh, my dear excellent girl! And how contemptible of me!' And she buried her face in her daughter's lap. The Marquise gasped in consternation: 'What is the matter, mother?' 'For let me tell you now,' continued her mother, 'that nothing of what I have been saying to you is true; you are purer than an angel, you radiate such innocence that my corrupted soul could not believe in it, and I could not convince myself of it without descending to this shameful trick.' 'My dearest mother!' cried the Marquise, full of happy emotion, and stooped down to her, trying to raise her to her feet. But her mother said: 'No, I shall not move from your feet, you splendid, heavenly creature, until you tell me that you can forgive the baseness of my behaviour.' 'Am *I* to forgive *you*!' exclaimed her daughter. 'Please rise, I do implore you—' 'You heard me,' said the Commandant's wife. 'I want to know whether you can still love me, whether you can still respect me as sincerely as ever?' 'My adored mother!' cried the Marquise, now kneeling before her as well, 'my heart has never lost any of its respect and love for you. Under such extraordinary circumstances, how was it possible for anyone to trust me? How glad I am that you are convinced that I have done nothing wrong!' 'Well, my dearest child,' said her mother, standing up with her daughter's assistance, 'now I shall love and cherish you. You shall have your confinement in my house; and I shall treat you with no less tenderness and respect than if we had reason to expect your baby to be a young prince. I shall never desert you now as long as I live. I defy the whole world; I *want* no greater honour than your shame—if only you will love me again, and forget the hardhearted way in which I rejected you!' The Marquise tried to comfort her with endless caresses and assurances, but evening fell and midnight struck before she had succeeded. Next day, when the old lady had recovered a little from her emotion, which had made her feverish during the night, the mother, daughter and grandchildren drove back in triumph, as it were, to M——. Their journey was a very happy one, and they joked about the groom Leopardo as he sat in front of them driving the carriage: the Marquise's mother said she noticed how her daughter blushed every time she looked at his broad shoulders, and the Marquise, reacting half with a sigh and half with a smile, answered: 'I wonder after all who the man will be who turns up at our house on the morning of the third!' Then, the nearer they got to M——, the more serious their mood became again, in anticipation of the crucial scenes that still awaited them. As soon as they had arrived at the house, the Commandant's wife, concealing her plans, showed her daughter back to her old rooms, and told her to make herself comfortable; then, saying that she would soon be back, she slipped away. An hour later she returned with her face very flushed. 'Why, what a doubting Thomas!' she said, though she seemed secretly delighted, 'what a doubting

47

Thomas! Didn't I need a whole hour by the clock to convince him! But now he's sitting there weeping.' 'Who!' asked the Marquise. 'He himself,' answered her mother. 'Who else but the person with the most cause for it!' 'Surely not my father?' exclaimed the Marquise. 'Weeping like a child,' replied her mother. 'If I had not had to wipe the tears out of my own eyes, I should have burst out laughing as soon as I got outside the door.' 'And all this on my account?' asked her daughter, rising to her feet, 'and you expect me to stay here and—?' 'You shall not budge!' said her mother. 'Why did he dictate that letter to me! *He* shall come here to *you*, or I shall have no more to do with him as long as I live.' 'My dearest mother—' pleaded the Marquise, but her mother interrupted her. 'I'll not give way! Why did he reach for that pistol?' 'But I implore you—' 'You *shall* not go to him,' replied the Commandant's wife, forcing her daughter to sit down again, 'and if he does not come by this evening, I shall leave the house with you tomorrow.' The Marquise said that this would be a hard and unfair way to act, but her mother answered (for she could already hear sobs approaching from a distance): 'You need not worry; here he is already!' 'Where?' asked her daughter, and sat listening. 'Is there someone there at the door, quite convulsed with—?' 'Of course!' replied the Commandant's wife; 'he wants us to open it for him.' 'Let me go!' cried the Marquise, leaping from her chair. But her mother answered: 'Giulietta, if you love me, stay where you are!'— and at that very moment the Commandant entered the room, holding his handkerchief to his face. His wife placed herself

48

directly between him and her daughter and turned her back on him. 'My dearest father!' cried the Marquise, stretching out her arms towards him. 'You shall not budge, I tell you!' said her mother. The Commandant stood there in the room, weeping. 'He is to apologize to you,' continued his wife. 'Why has he such a violent temper, and why is he so obstinate? I love him but I love you too; I respect him, but I respect you too. And if I must choose, then you are a finer person than him, and I shall stay with you.' The Commandant was standing bent almost double and weeping so loudly that the walls re-echoed. 'Oh, my God, but—' exclaimed the Marquise, suddenly giving up the struggle with her mother, and taking out her handkerchief to let her own tears flow. Her mother said: 'It's just that he can't speak!' and moved a little to one side. At this the Marquise rose, embraced her father, and begged him to calm himself. She too was weeping profusely. She asked him if he would not sit down, and tried to draw him on to a chair; she pushed one up for him to sit on; but he made no answer, he could not be induced to move, nor even sit down, but merely stood there with his face bowed low over the ground, and wept. The Marquise, holding him upright, half turned to her mother and said she thought he would make himself ill; her mother too seemed on the point of losing her composure, for he was going almost into convulsions. But when he had finally seated himself, yielding to the repeated pleas of his daughter, and the latter, ceaselessly caressing him, had sunk down at his feet, his wife returned to her point, declared that it served him right, and that now he would no doubt come to his senses; whereupon she departed and left the two of them in the room.

As soon as she was outside the door she wiped away her own tears, wondering whether the violent emotional upheaval she had caused him might not after all be dangerous, and whether it would be advisable to have a doctor called. She went to the kitchen and cooked for his dinner all the most nourishing and comforting dishes she could devise; she prepared and warmed his bed, intending to put him into it as soon as, hand in hand with his daughter, he reappeared. But when the dinner table was already laid and there was still no sign of him, she crept back to the Marquise's room to find out what on earth was going on. Putting her ear gently against the door and listening, she caught the last echo of some softly murmured words, spoken, as it seemed to her, by the Marquise; and looking through the keyhole she noticed that her daughter was even sitting on the Commandant's lap, a thing he had never before permitted. And when finally she opened the door she saw a sight that made her heart leap with joy: her daughter, with her head thrown right back and her eyes tightly shut, was lying quietly in her father's arms, while the latter, with tears glistening in his wide-open eyes, sat in the armchair, pressing long, ardent, avid kisses on to her mouth, just like a lover! His daughter said nothing, he said nothing; he sat with his face bowed over her, as if she were the first girl he had ever loved; he sat there holding her mouth near his and kissing her. Her mother felt quite transported with delight; standing unseen behind his chair, she hesitated to interrupt this blissful scene of reconciliation which had brought such joy back to her house. Finally, she approached her husband, and just as he was again stroking and kissing his daughter's mouth in indescribable ecstasy, she leaned round the side of the chair and looked at him. When the Commandant saw her he at once lowered his eyes again with a cross expression and was about to say something; but she exclaimed: 'Oh, what a face to make!' And then she in her turn smoothed it out with kisses, and talked jestingly until the atmosphere of emotion was dispelled. She asked them both to come and have dinner, and as she led the way they walked along like a pair of betrothed lovers; at table the Commandant seemed very happy, though he still sobbed from time to time, ate and spoke little, gazed down at his plate, and caressed his daughter's hand.

The question now was, who in the world would turn up at eleven o'clock on the following morning, for the next day to dawn would be the dreaded third. The Marquise's father and mother, as well as her brother who had arrived to share in the general reconciliation, were decidedly in favour of marriage, if the person should be at least tolerably acceptable; everything within the realm of possibility would be done to ensure her happiness. If, on the other hand, the circumstances of the person in question should turn out to be such that even with the help of her family they would still fall too short of the Marquise's own, then her parents were opposed to her marrying him; they were resolved in that case to let her live with them as before and to adopt the child as theirs. It seemed, however, to be the Marquise's wish to keep her promise in any case, provided the person were not a complete scoundrel, and thus at all costs to provide the child with a father. On the eve of the assignation her mother raised the question of how the visitor was to be received. The Commandant was of the opinion that the most suitable procedure would be, when eleven o'clock came, to leave the Marquise by herself. The latter however insisted that both her parents, and her brother as well, should be present, since she did not want to share any secrets with the expected person. She also thought that this would be his own wish, which in his answer he had seemed to express by suggesting her father's house as the place for the meeting; and she added that she must confess to having been greatly pleased by this answer for that very reason. Her mother thought that under this arrangement the roles played by her husband and son would be most unseemly; she begged her daughter to consent to the two men being absent, but agreed to meet her wishes to the extent of being present herself when the person arrived. After the Marquise had thought it over for a little this last proposal was finally adopted. The night was then passed in a state of suspense and expectancy, and now the morning of the dreaded third had come. As the clock struck eleven both women were sitting in the reception room, festively attired as for a betrothal; their hearts were beating so hard that one could have heard them if the noises of daytime had ceased. The eleventh stroke of the clock was still reverberating when

Leopardo entered, the groom whom the Commandment had hired from Tyrol. At the sight of him the women turned pale. 'I am to announce Count F—, my lady,' he said, 'his carriage is at the door.' 'Count F—!' they exclaimed simultaneously, thrown from one kind of consternation into another. The Marquise cried: 'Shut the doors! We are not at home to him!' She rose at once to lock the door of the room herself, and was in the act of thrusting out the groom as he stood in her way, when the Count entered, in exactly the same uniform, with the same decorations and weapons, as he had worn and carried on the day of the storming of the fortress. The Marquise felt she would sink into the ground from sheer confusion; she snatched up a handkerchief she had left lying on her chair and was about to rush off into a neighbouring room, when her mother, seizing her by the hand, exclaimed: 'Giulietta—!', and her thoughts seemed to stifle any further words. She stared straight at the Count, and repeated, drawing her daughter towards her: 'Why, Giulietta, whom have we been expecting—?' The Marquise, turning suddenly, cried, 'Well? You surely cannot mean him—?' She fixed on the Count such a look that it seemed to flash like a thunderbolt, and her face went deathly pale. He had gone down on one knee before her; his right hand was on his heart, his head meekly bowed, and there he remained, blushing scarlet and with downcast eyes, saying nothing. 'Who else?' exclaimed her mother, her voice almost failing. 'Who else but him? How stupid we have been—!' The Marquise stood over him, rigidly erect, and said: 'Mother, I shall go mad!' 'Foolish girl,' replied her mother, and drew her towards her and whispered something into her ear. The Marquise turned away and collapsed on to the sofa with both hands pressed against her face. Her mother cried: 'Poor wretched girl! What is the matter with you? What has happened that can have taken you by surprise?' The Count did not move, but knelt on beside the Commandant's wife, and taking the outermost hem of her dress in his hand he kissed it. 'Dear, gracious, noble lady!' he whispered, and a tear rolled down his cheek. 'Stand up, Count,' she answered, 'stand up! Comfort my daughter; then we shall all be reconciled, and all will be forgiven and forgotten.' The Count rose to his feet, still shedding tears. He again knelt down in front of the Marquise, gently took her hand as if it were made of gold and the warmth of his own might tarnish it. But she, standing up, cried: 'Go away! go away! go away! I was prepared to meet a vicious man, but not—not a devil!' And so saying she moved away from him as if he were a person infected with the plague, threw open the door of the room and said: 'Call my father!' 'Giuletta!' cried her mother in astonishment. The Marquise stared at them each in turn with annihilating rage; her breast heaved, her face was aflame; no Fury's gaze could be more terrifying. The Commandant and his son arrived. 'Father,' said the Marquise, as they were in the act of entering the room, 'I cannot marry this man!' And dipping her hand into a vessel of holy water that was fastened to the door, she scattered it lavishly over her father, mother and brother, and fled.

The Commandant, disconcerted by this strange occurrence, asked what had happened, and turned pale when he noticed that Count F— was in the room at this decisive moment. His wife took the Count by the hand and said: 'Do not ask; this young man sincerely repents all that has happened; give him your blessing, give it, give it—and all will still turn out for the best.' The Count stood there utterly mortified. The Commandant laid his hand on his head; his eyelids twitched, his lips were as white as chalk. 'May the curse of heaven be averted from your head!' he exclaimed. 'When are you intending to get married?' 'Tomorrow,' answered the Marquise's mother on the Count's behalf, for the latter was unable to utter a word. 'Tomorrow or today, whichever you like; I am sure no time will be too soon for my lord the Count, who has shown such admirable zeal to make amends for his wrongdoing.' 'Then I shall have the pleasure of seeing you tomorrow at eleven o'clock at the Church of St Augustine!' said the Commandant; whereupon he bowed to him, asked his wife and son to accompany him to his daughter's room, and left the Count to himself.

The family made vain efforts to discover from the Marquise the reason for her strange behaviour; she was lying in an acutely feverish condition, refused absolutely to listen to any talk of getting married, and asked them to leave her alone. When they inquired why she had suddenly changed her mind and what made the Count more repugnant to her than any other suitor, she gave her father a blank wide-eyed stare and made no answer. Her mother asked whether she had forgotten that she was herself a mother; to which she replied that in the present case she was bound to consider her own interests before those of the child, and calling on all the angels and saints as witnesses she reasserted her refusal to marry. Her father, to whom it seemed obvious that she was in a hysterical state of mind, declared that she must keep her word; he then left her, and put in hand all the arrangements for the wedding after an appropriate written exchange with the Count. He submitted to him a marriage contract by which he would renounce all conjugal rights while at the same time binding himself to fulfil any duties that might be imposed upon him. The document came back wet with tears, bearing the Count's signature. When the Commandant handed it the next morning to the Marquise she had somewhat recovered her composure. Still sitting in her bed, she read the paper through several times, folded it up thoughtfully, opened it again and re-read it; then she declared that she would come to the Church of St Augustine at eleven o'clock. She rose, dressed without saying a word, got into the carriage with her parents and brother when the hour struck, and drove off to the appointed meeting-place.

The Count was not permitted to join the family until they reached the entrance to the church. During the ceremony the Marquise stared rigidly at the painting behind the altar and did not vouchsafe even a fleeting glance at the man with whom she was exchanging rings. When the marriage service ended, the Count offered her his arm; but as soon as they reached the church door again the Countess took her leave of him with a bow; her father inquired whether he would occasionally have the honour of seeing him in his daughter's apartments; whereupon the Count muttered something unintelligible, raising his hat to the company, and disappeared. He moved into a residence in M— and spent several months there without ever once setting foot in the Commandant's house, where the Countess continued to live. It was only owing to his delicate, dignified, and wholly exemplary behaviour on all occasions on which he came into any contact at all with the family, that when in due course the Countess was delivered of an infant son he was invited to the christening. The Countess, still confined and sitting in her bed under richly embroidered coverlets, saw him only for an instant when he presented himself and greeted her from a respectful distance. Among the other presents with which the guests had welcomed the newcomer, he threw on to his son's cradle two documents; after his departure one of these turned out to be a deed of gift of 20,000 roubles to the boy, and the other a will making the boy's mother, in the event of the Count's death, heiress to his entire fortune. From that day on the Commandant's wife saw to it that he was frequently invited; the house was open to him and soon not an evening passed without his paying the family a visit. His instinct told him that, in consideration of the imperfection inherent in the order of the world, he had been forgiven by all of them, and he therefore began a second wooing of the Countess, his wife; when a year had passed he won from her a second consent, and they even celebrated a second wedding, happier than the first, after which the whole family moved out to the estate at V—. A whole series of young Russians now followed the first, and during one happy hour the Count asked his wife why, on that terrible third day of the month, when she had seemed willing to receive the most vicious of debauchees, she had fled from him as if from a devil. Throwing her arms round his neck, she answered that she would not have seen a devil in him then if she had not seen an angel in him at their first meeting.

READ MORE IN PENGUIN

For complete information about books available from Penguin and how to order them, please write to us at the appropriate address below. Please note that for copyright reasons the selection of books varies from country to country.

IN THE UNITED KINGDOM: Please write to *Dept. JC, Penguin Books Ltd, FREEPOST, West Drayton, Middlesex UB7 0BR.*

If you have any difficulty in obtaining a title, please send your order with the correct money, plus ten per cent for postage and packaging, to *PO Box No. 11, West Drayton, Middlesex UB7 0BR.*

IN THE UNITED STATES: Please write to *Consumer Sales, Penguin USA, P.O. Box 999, Dept. 17109, Bergenfield, New Jersey 07621-0120.* VISA and MasterCard holders call 1-800-253-6476 to order all Penguin titles.

IN CANADA: Please write to *Penguin Books Canada Ltd, 10 Alcorn Avenue, Suite 300, Toronto, Ontario M4V 3B2.*

IN AUSTRALIA: Please write to *Penguin Books Australia Ltd, P.O. Box 257, Ringwood, Victoria 3134.*

IN NEW ZEALAND: Please write to *Penguin Books (NZ) Ltd, Private Bag 102902, North Shore Mail Centre, Auckland 10.*

IN INDIA: Please write to *Penguin Books India Pvt Ltd, 706 Eros Apartments, 56 Nehru Place, New Delhi 110 019.*

IN THE NETHERLANDS: Please write to *Penguin Books Netherlands bv, Postbus 3507, NL-1001 AH Amsterdam.*

IN GERMANY: Please write to *Penguin Books Deutschland GmbH, Metzlerstrasse 26, 60594 Frankfurt am Main.*

IN SPAIN: Please write to *Penguin Books S. A., Bravo Murillo 19, 1o B, 28015 Madrid.*

IN ITALY: Please write to *Penguin Italia s.r.l., Via Felice Casati 20, I-20124 Milano.*

IN FRANCE: Please write to *Penguin France S. A., 17 rue Lejeune, F-31000 Toulouse.*

IN JAPAN: Please write to *Penguin Books Japan, Ishikiribashi Building, 2-5-4, Suido, Bunkyo-ku, Tokyo 112.*

IN GREECE: Please write to *Penguin Hellas Ltd, Dimocritou 3, GR-106 71 Athens.*

IN SOUTH AFRICA: Please write to *Longman Penguin Southern Africa (Pty) Ltd, Private Bag X08, Bertsham 2013.*